. . . *for parents and teachers*

Will Dad Ever Move Back Home? presents many of the emotions experienced by children in divorcing families — including guilt and responsibility for the breakup, alienation and anger toward parents, and the desire to reunite the family. It also includes realistic life changes, such as added household responsibilities and lack of high-quality time with either parent.

As Laura in this story is able to communicate her underlying feelings of loneliness and guilt more directly, her parents respond more appropriately both to her needs and their own.

This ability to express feelings is often the crux of successful coping in a family divorce situation.

MARTHA F. MUIR, Ph.D.
COUNSELING PSYCHOLOGY
MILWAUKEE, WISCONSIN

Library of Congress Number: 79-24058

7 8 9 10 11 12   93 92 91 90 89 88 87

Printed in the United States of America.

Library of Congress Cataloging in Publication Data

Hogan, Paula Z.
    Will dad ever move back home?

    SUMMARY: When a child is bitterly unhappy that her
divorced parents no longer live together, she and her
family discover the importance of her directly expressing
her feelings.
    (1. Divorce - Fiction) I. Leder, Dora. II. Title.
PZ7.H68313Wi   (Fic)   79-24058
ISBN 0-8172-1356-2 lib. bdg.

WILL DAD EVER MOVE BACK HOME?

by *Paula Z. Hogan*

illustrated by Dora Leder

introduction by Martha F. Muir, Ph.D.

RAINTREE CHILDRENS BOOKS
Milwaukee

Sometimes my house is so quiet I can't stand it.

One Tuesday I came home from school and just wandered from room to room, looking for something to do. Finally I climbed up on the sofa and jumped up and down. Mom screams if she sees me doing that. But Mom wasn't home yet. And my brother John was at his Boy Scout meeting.

Sometimes my house is so quiet I can't stand it.

4

When Mom finally did come home, she was in kind of a bad mood.

"You haven't set the table yet, Laura," she said. "I'll bet you didn't fold the wash either."

"I'm sorry, Mom. I guess I forgot." To myself I was thinking, *Boy, I'm glad she didn't see me jumping on the sofa*!

"Laura, how many times do I have to tell you? Now that I'm working, you and John have to help around the house more. I don't have time to do everything."

I rushed around setting the table, thinking about Mom and Dad. They don't live together anymore, and it's driving me crazy.

"Oh, why did Dad have to move out?" I thought to myself. "Of course, he still takes us places and buys us things. But it's not the same. I liked it better when we were a real family."

I was wishing I could have said those things to Mom. But she gets kind of touchy when the subject of Dad comes up.

After supper I wandered into John's room. He was supposed to be doing his homework, but he was working on his model airplanes instead.

"Did you have a good time with Dad last Saturday?" I asked.

"Fantastic. We went to the car races. Where is he taking you this Saturday?"

That was the deal we had — John and I took turns spending Saturdays with Dad.

"Ice skating," I answered. "Want to see the skates he bought me? They're really. . ."

"Maybe later," John said as he bent over an airplane. "I'm busy."

I knew he was hinting for me to leave, but I sat down on his bed anyway. "Do you think Dad will ever move back home?" I asked him.

"No."

"Even if we were real good?"

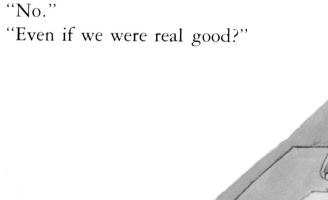

"I don't think *we* have anything to do with it," John said. "Mom and Dad were always fighting about stuff that didn't have anything to do with us."

"I know, but I still think —"

"I'm busy," John said again.

This time I took the hint. It bothered
me that John didn't seem to care as much
as I did about Dad's moving out. I had
noticed, though, that John was spending
more and more time on his airplanes lately,
and less and less time on his schoolwork.

Early Saturday morning I got ready to go ice skating.

"I'm going to my class now," Mom called. "Make sure your father brings you home on time."

"Wait a minute!" I said. "Aren't you going to be here when Dad comes to pick me up?"

"No, why?"

"I . . . I thought maybe you could talk to him. And maybe then you could make up."

"Oh, Laura." Mom sat down. "Your dad and I weren't happy when we lived together. We'd just start fighting again if he moved back here. I know how bad you feel. I feel bad too. But things are better this way. Maybe it doesn't seem better right now, but just give it a chance. You'll see."

I got mad. "I just wanted us to be a real family again, and you won't even try!"

Mom didn't say anything. That *really* bothers me — when she doesn't talk to me, as if I'm too little to understand what's going on.

I picked up my skates and ran outside to wait for Dad.

We had such a good time at the skating rink that I forgot all about my fight with Mom.

I kept skating faster and faster. "Try and catch me, Dad," I shouted.

Dad was close behind me. He reached out to grab me, when . . . *clunk*! Down we fell. We were laughing so hard that we couldn't get up at first.

Finally Dad stood up. "Come on, let's get something to eat. Where would you like to go?"

I pointed. "How about that hamburger place over there?"

Minutes later, I was biting into a juicy hamburger. "We sure have a good time together," I said. "Don't we, Dad?"

He smiled at me.

I got an idea. "Dad, could I move in with you?" I asked.

"Why would you want to do that?"

"Because I have so much more fun with you. Mom is always too busy and tired to have fun."

"If you lived with me," he said, "you'd find out how busy and tired I am most of the time too. Anyway, your mother decided that she wanted to take care of you and John. Maybe later we can all change our minds about it. But I think we should give this plan more of a chance, don't you?"

Very quietly I said, "You don't want me to live with you."

"That's not true, and you know it." Dad looked at his watch. "It's late. Finish your hamburger, and I'll take you home."

"I'm not hungry," I mumbled. "Let's go."

By the next morning I had made up my mind about what to do. I got up earlier than anyone else. I tiptoed downstairs and out the back door.

When I walked past the playground, I saw two of my friends, Jeff and Mark. I waved but didn't stop to talk.

"Hey, Laura," called Jeff. "Come here— we're playing spaceship."

"Can't," I called back. "I'm running away." To myself I added, *I'm running away because both of my parents hate me*. But I didn't say that out loud.

19

Jeff and Mark chased after me.

"Neat," said Mark. "Where are you going?"

"I haven't decided yet. Somewhere where I can be alone."

"How about that old house on Elm Street?" said Mark. "Nobody has lived there for a long time."

"Thanks for the tip," I said. "And please don't tell anyone you told me." Then I ran down the street.

I knew what house Mark was talking about — the one with the peeling paint and the boards over the windows. The one with the Keep Out sign in front of it.

I stood on the porch for a long time, trying to get up the courage to go inside. Finally I tried the front door. It was locked.

So was the back door. By now I had decided I really wanted to get inside. So I searched until I found an open basement window. Then I wiggled through it.

Thump! It was a lot further to the floor than I had guessed. I felt lucky I was still in one piece.

I took my time exploring the dark and
dusty basement. Empty jars, broken
furniture, and cobwebs were everywhere.
It was too spooky for me, so I decided to
go upstairs. One by one I climbed the
creaky stairs.

But when I tried to open the door at the
top of the stairs, it wouldn't budge.

"Oh, no," I whispered. "How am I ever
going to get out of here? That window's
much too high for me to climb out the
way I came."

Just then, there was a bumping noise on
the other side of the door. I heard it
coming closer . . . . closer to the door.

"Laura . . . Laura," called a voice.

"It's coming to get me!" I gasped. I raced down the stairs toward the window.
Crash!
Something tripped me.
Before I could get up, the basement door opened. Dark figures stood at the top of the stairs.
I screamed.

"Laura, is that you?"
It was Mom and Dad! I ran to them, crying, "Something tried to get me!"
"It was just us and the caretaker," said Dad, holding me close.
"We've been looking all over for you," said Mom. "Some kids at the playground told us you might be here."
"You could hurt yourself in a place like this," Dad said. "Are you all right?"
"Y-Yes," I said. "And I'm never coming back here again!"

Slowly we walked back to our house.

Dad took my hand. "Your mother and I were talking about you this morning," he said. "We know how much our divorce upsets you. We think that it would make us all feel better if I saw you more often. Would you and John like to come to my apartment one night each week? We'll make dinner and talk, and you could sleep overnight. What do you think?"

"I'd like that," I said. "Can we go to exciting places every week?"

Dad shook his head. "From now on we're saving movies and other trips for special treats."

"What about Saturdays?" I asked.

"You and John can each take turns spending Saturdays with me, just like always. But instead of going places, we'll stay around home. I . . . I think it's fun just being together, don't you?"

I nodded happily. Then I kissed him good-bye and went into the house with Mom.

"I still don't have a real family," I said to Mom.

"You have a different kind of a family," she said. "What counts is that your father and I both love you. That stays the same, even though other things have changed."

"Thanks, Mom. Should I go fold the wash now?"

"Why don't we just sit down for a while?" she said. "I think we have a lot to talk about."

"Okay," I said and gave her a big hug.